DATE DUE			
			FEB 8 1996

Moonsnail Song

Sheryl McFarlane ~ Sheena Lott

Moonsnail Song

ORCA BOOK PUBLISHERS

APRIL has a hidden treasure.

It sings her to the sea.

Her moonsnail sings of tidal flats,
of water-rippled sandy shores
and otter rolling in swaying kelp.
It whispers of the misty morning fogs,
and sea salt air.

Her moonsnail sings a harmony
of sideways scuttling crabs
and driftwood tangles on the rocks,
of crying gulls and crashing waves
beating out their rhythm against the rocky shore.
In and out.
Out and in.

Like the rhythm of April's feet on the sidewalk
as she skips rope in the park.
Like the rhythm of her heartbeat
as she skips her way to school.

And later April daydreams at her desk.
Her fingertips follow moonsnail whorls to hermit crabs
and tidepool sculpin,
sea urchins and much more,
barnacles, anemones and a dozen different sea stars.

Without moving she has come to her favourite rocky shore,
where frothy spray reaches for the jutting cliffs
and a solitary raven's call
is barely heard above the pounding of the sea.

After dinner April traces moonsnail patterns
on the table that she wipes,
while the steady muffled bass of her brother's music
beats out the rhythm of the sea.
In and out.
Out and in.

Salt water ripples gently over sand
and April searches for a moonsnail.
She stoops to touch a slippery eggcase
made of slime and sand and a million unhatched eggs.
Although moonsnails elude her,
she finds a shell to bring back home.

The phone is ringing.
Hurried footsteps thump down stairs,
but April hardly hears.
Do moonsnails feel the tides
under all that sand and mud?
she wonders.

Later, as twilight cloaks her street,
April lingers in the bath.
Her fingers trace the spirals of her shell
and she is almost there,
carried on the whorls of her moonsnail,
like a scoter on the surf.

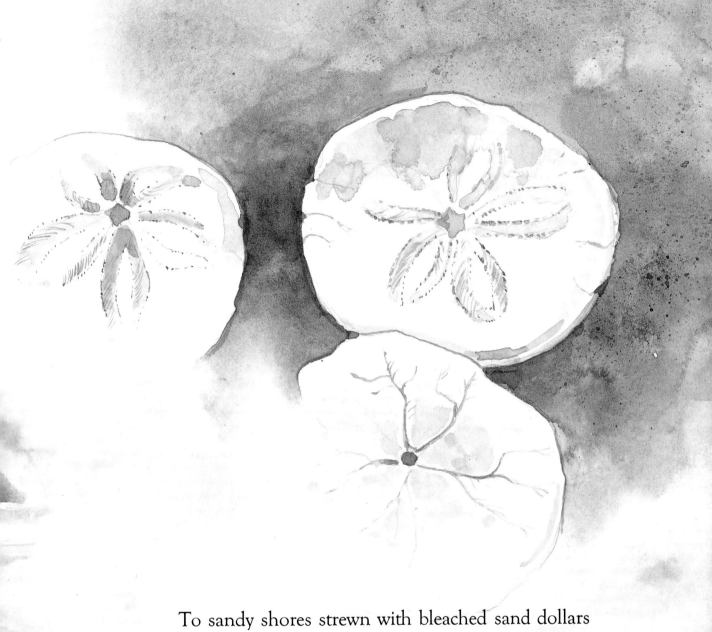

To sandy shores strewn with bleached sand dollars
of delicate design
and stranded jellyfish pale as moonlight.

To oyster beds piled ankle deep,
and swaying strands of eelgrass
hiding shrimp and snails and ghostly nudibranchs.

The music of her feet slapping summer sand is
a plover's nimble dance
keeping time with gentle lapping waves.
In and out.
Out and in.

The ocean keeps its rhythmic beat
from dawn to dusk and dusk to dawn.
In and out.
Out and in.
The ripples of her bath sing April's ocean song.

From April's bedroom window
the breeze plays on her skin.
Her moonsnail shell sings softly of pale moonlight
and phosphorescent midnight seas,
and she can almost smell the sea fresh air.
Whispering maples gently sway outside her window,
while April drifts in and out of sleep.

Moonlit bats flutter by,
swooping through arbutus trees,
catching insects on the wing
as they ride the offshore breeze.
In and out.
Out and in.

The ocean sings its lapping song.
In and out.
Out and in.
Whispers April's sleeping song,
from dusk to dawn,
April dreams the sea.

To all the daydreamers
whose imaginations have
led them up familiar paths
or down new roads
S.M.

To Ian, Alison, Fiona, Rita and Joe
May all your dreams of the ocean
come true
S.L.

Text copyright © 1994 Sheryl McFarlane
Illustration copyright © 1994 Sheena Lott

Publication assistance provided by The Canada Council
All rights reserved

Canadian Cataloguing in Publication Data
McFarlane, Sheryl, 1954 –
Moonsnail song

ISBN 1-55143-008-8
II. Lott, Sheena, 1950 –   II. Title.
PS8575.F39M6 1994   jX813'.54   C94-910026-9
PZ7.M32Mo 1994

Design by Christine Toller
Printed and bound in the Republic of Korea

Orca Book Publishers
PO Box 5626, Station B
Victoria, BC V8R 6S4
Canada

Orca Book Publishers
#3028, 1574 Gulf Road
Point Roberts, WA 98281
USA